SHARING MY SEDUCTIVE HOT WIFE

WIFE SHARING HOTWIFE EROTICA COLLECTION

WIFE SHARING FANTASIES
BOOK TWO

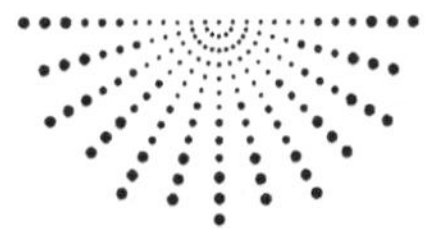

LEE RILEY

SHARING MY WIFE AT THE OFFICE

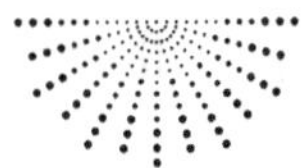

* * *

I want you in my office in an hour," Kyle said sternly. "And you'll need to bring the discipline bag."

Megan's hand trembled as she held the phone to her ear. When she'd overdrawn the checking account a few weeks ago she'd known that there would be a day of reckoning, and based on her husband's tone of voice, that day had come.

"Yes, sir," she managed to whisper before he disconnected.

After two years of practicing Domestic Discipline in their marriage, Megan was well trained. She didn't even consider disobeying her husband's command. She had agreed that he was the Head of Household, and she submitted to his authority in all aspects of their life.

She knew she'd earned whatever punishment he had in store for her, but the fact that he was going to give it to her now, in the middle of his work day, rather than waiting until he got home made her nervous. It suggested that she'd be walking stiffly for a few days at least, and her bottom had already started to tingle in anticipation.

Kyle worked about twenty minutes away, and Megan took a little time to freshen up before leaving. She fixed her hair and makeup, and changed into a demure dress appropriate for the wife of a senior partner at her husband's prestigious firm. There was no way she was going to embarrass him by showing up looking less than her best.

Per Kyle's instructions, she grabbed the discipline bag as she headed out the door. Just the thought of what was inside made her heart start to pound. It also reminded her that she'd probably end up with her face as red as her bottom, and streaked with tears, so she wasted precious minutes going back into the house to grab her makeup and a compact mirror to fix herself up after he was done with her.

* * *

"Hi, Megan," Kyle's perky young secretary greeted her as she walked in. "He's expecting you."

"Thanks, Sharon," Megan replied with a shaky smile.

"He asked me to clear his calendar this afternoon," the girl told her with a suggestive wink. "I think that's so sweet!"

Megan just nodded as she walked past Sharon's desk. "Sweet" was not a word that she'd apply to her husband, and that was fine with her. Even though she knew that he was about to cause her some serious pain, the truth was that she appreciated the fact that he cared enough to discipline her.

Kyle was more attentive than most husbands, to hear her friends talk. He always knew what she was doing, and what she needed, sometimes better than she did herself. Megan loved that about him, and was happy to treat him with the respect and obedience that he deserved for taking such good care of her.

She took a deep breath and walked into his office, closing the door behind her. No matter how much she agreed with it in theory, though, the moment that she had to bend over and bare her bottom was never fun.

"Lock it, Pumpkin," Kyle directed her as he came around from behind his desk to greet her.

"Yes, sir," she responded automatically.

He took the discipline bag and her purse from her and set them on his credenza before pulling her in for a kiss. As always, Megan's knees went a little weak at the touch of his firm lips. Kyle pulled her closer, his large hand sliding down over her ass and pressing her against his groin.

"I had to cancel some important meetings this afternoon," he murmured against her mouth. "That's another thing you'll have to answer for today." Kyle ground his stiffening cock against her stomach, leaving her no doubt about how he expected her to make up for disrupting his work day.

Megan had hoped he had more in mind than just a spanking, but she hadn't wanted to presume. Now that she knew she had something to look forward to, she wanted nothing more than to get on with it. Her pussy was already wet.

"Tom Wilder flew in last night to handle the Martinez case," Kyle told her as he pulled away.

Megan looked at him in confusion. Tom's name was vaguely familiar to her, but Kyle rarely talked to her in any detail about his work. She wasn't sure why he brought it up now, when all she wanted to do was bend over and take her punishment.

"He and I were supposed to wrap up the final details this afternoon, and he wasn't happy when I told him I'd have to postpone."

Oh. Crap. She could tell Kyle wasn't happy about that, but Megan had to admit that part of her was thrilled to know that he took his responsibilities as her husband so seriously.

"Is there, um, any way I can make it up to you, honey?" she asked, tentatively placing a hand on his chest as she looked up at him.

"Maybe," Kyle answered with a sigh. He stepped back and ran a hand through his hair. "Tom's become a good friend. In fact, when I had to fly back east a couple of months ago for the board meeting, he and his wife had me over to dinner."

"That's nice, honey," she replied. "You work so hard, it's great that you were able to relax a little bit on that trip."

Kyle nodded, glancing down at his watch. "It turns out that we have quite a bit in common. Including living a Domestic Discipline lifestyle."

Megan raised her eyebrows in surprise. She and Kyle didn't often share their lifestyle choice with others, not even close friends and family. Most people simply didn't understand how she could "let" him spank and punish her, and they'd both agreed that other people's ignorant attitudes could affect his career. Just another reason to keep it quiet.

"While I was there, Tom's wife, Susan, was punished for being disrespectful. Tom didn't know my own feelings on the matter at the time, and I admired the fact that he didn't hesitate to discipline her just because I was visiting. I told him so afterward, and once he knew that I understood, he offered to have her make it up to me since I was the one she disrespected."

Megan's breath hitched. Make it up to him? She wasn't sure what that meant, but if it was anything like their own style of Domestic Discipline she wasn't sure that she liked the sound of it. Not that it was her place to question her husband.

"Anyway," Kyle continued. "I thought I would offer Tom the same courtesy, since your actions have inconvenienced him this time."

A knock sounded on the door as Megan tried to process his words. What did he mean? Was he going to… let Tom punish her? Or have her make it up to him some other way?

"Thanks for coming by, Tom," Kyle was saying to the distinguished looking man who had just walked in. "This is my wife, Megan."

Megan smiled at him automatically, dropping her eyes out of respect.

"She's beautiful, Kyle," Tom said appreciatively, walking around her to get a good look. "And I'm impressed that you take your responsibilities as her husband so seriously."

Megan couldn't help preening a little as Tom praised her. She loved being seen as a credit to her man.

"Okay Pumpkin," Kyle told her. "It's time to pay the piper. I was just waiting for Tom to arrive, but you know there's no more putting off the inevitable."

"Yes, sir," Megan replied obediently. She'd actually let herself get distracted and had forgotten for a moment what she still had to face.

"Take your clothes off, Meg," Kyle ordered as he walked over to lock his office door

"A-all of them, sir?" she asked with a nervous glance at Tom. She'd worn a dress to give him easy access, assuming he would want her to stay mostly covered since he'd be punishing her in the work place. Apparently she was wrong.

Kyle's brows lowered at her backtalk, and she realized she'd just embarrassed him in front of Tom.

"Yes, sir," she said, blushing. She quickly stripped off her dress, panties, and bra.

"Leave them," Kyle said as she reached for the tops of her black stockings.

Megan nodded, glancing at Tom out of the corner of her eye. She was shocked that her possessive husband was allowing another man to see her naked, but she had to admit that a small part of her found it exciting. Tom was staring at her full breasts with a very appreciative smile, and instantly her nipples hardened into tight pebbles.

"Bend over the desk," Kyle directed her while he retrieved the discipline bag.

Megan folded her arms under her head on the rich wood of her husband's desk and spread her legs, arching her back to present her curvy ass for punishment. She could no longer see the men, and she couldn't help tensing a little as she wondered if

Kyle was going to let Tom punish her, or just have the other man watch. Within moments, she got her answer.

"Would you like to warm her up for me, Tom?" Kyle asked the other man. "She's earned more than just a bare hand, but that will do to start."

"Happy to help," Tom answered cheerfully.

Megan had never been spanked by anyone but her husband, and when Tom's hand connected with her bottom for the first time she gasped. He used more force than she was used to, at least for a warm up, and it shot stinging tendrils of erotic excitement through her lower body. Megan didn't usually react that way to a spanking, and she wasn't sure if it was the fact that a strange man had his hands on her, or his technique.

"Spread your legs wider, Megan," Tom ordered with authority.

She automatically complied, and then sucked in a quick breath as she wondered what Kyle would think to see her obeying another man so readily. Kyle had been the one to invite Tom's participation, she reminded herself, relaxing slightly. He would expect her to obey the other man.

Tom started to work her over thoroughly, alternating between her two cheeks and the sensitive tops of her thighs. Now that her legs were open so wide, every smack brought his fingers in contact with her wet pussy. Several times he spanked her right on the sensitized flesh, but mostly he just brushed against it as he reddened her.

Megan's ass was starting to burn, but it was nothing compared to the tension coiling between her legs. She bit her lip, trying to contain her excitement. It didn't seem right to get so turned on by another man, but she couldn't help it.

Tom suddenly spanked her pussy again, smack in the middle, and without meaning to Megan moaned. Tom did it again. He started spanking her, fast and hard, directly on her wet cunt, again and again.

She could hear both men breathing hard, but she couldn't concentrate on anything but the hot throbbing need between her legs. The rough treatment had her pushing back against Tom's hand with every smack, wantonly rubbing herself against him. If Tom kept it up she was going to come, hard, and embarrass her husband all over again.

"Tom," Kyle finally grunted in a strained voice. "Wait."

Breathing hard, Tom stepped away. Megan whimpered, and bit her lip in embarrassment.

She could hear her husband moving behind her, and then Tom walked around to the side of the desk where she could see him. His eyes were glued to her ass and he didn't notice her watching him. He looked disheveled and flushed, as if he had really been giving it his all. The sight excited her even more, and she wondered if Kyle would want the other man to continue to punish her.

Without warning, Megan heard the telltale whoosh of the paddle and then felt the hot burn as her husband cracked it against her warm ass. She'd been distracted, watching Tom, and it caught her off guard. She gasped and flinched away.

"Meg!"

Her husband's reprimand reminded her to hold still and take her punishment. He swung the paddle down again with a loud crack. The pain was intense, and it should have taken her mind off of her inappropriate arousal from Tom's spanking. But it didn't.

As her husband continued to paddle her, Megan kept her eyes on Tom. Specifically, she watched as the bulge in his pants stiffened and grew. Kyle didn't hold back, and the burning pain from the hard wooden plank became intense. Megan cried out, unable to hold back her tears as he laid into her. Through it all, though, her pussy continued to throb with desire.

Kyle often fucked her after he spanked her, and he'd all but promised her that when she'd arrived. Megan held on to that thought as the paddling went on and on.

"Are you going to cane her?" Tom asked in a husky voice, his hand stealing down to stroke his tented pants.

Kyle paused, giving Megan's red flanks time for the burn to really settle in. Her lower body felt like it was on fire, but somehow that just made her sexual tension all the more unbearable.

"I remember the welts you left on Susan," Kyle said to the other man. "You were a master of technique. I still remember how you laid them down in a perfectly even row across her ass."

Megan frowned at the idea of Tom admiring another woman's bare ass.

"I've found that welts serve as a good reminder, long after the punishment is over," Tom replied. "Would you mind if I... ?"

Kyle must have nodded, because Tom walked behind her again, where she couldn't see him. After a moment Megan heard the distinctive whistle of the cane singing through the air. It kissed her ass with a tongue of fire, and the burning touch was immediately followed by another, and another.

Each time, the sting was almost sensual for a split second, and then it blossomed into a burning stripe that consumed her attention. Megan couldn't help crying out with each stroke, even as part of her reveled in being marked. She wondered if striping her ass was making his cock harder, and whether her husband would allow him to do anything about it.

Finally, Tom stopped.

"Beautiful," he said approvingly, running a warm hand over her curvy bottom and making her shiver. "Are you satisfied?" he asked Tom.

Megan tensed. If this had purely been a punishment for the overdrawn checking account, she would expect her husband to say yes. But there was more at stake here than simply correcting her error with the household finances.

She had disrupted his business routine, and also inconvenienced Tom. She'd embarrassed her husband, and as much as her bottom burned right now, she knew she'd lose a little respect for him if he let her get away without paying the price in full.

Kyle didn't disappoint her.

"No," he said to Tom. And then, to Megan: "Stand up, Pumpkin, and turn around."

Megan did, her throbbing backside causing her to move stiffly.

"Tom, would you please restrain her hands behind her?" Kyle asked politely.

Megan could see that Tom's cock was still standing at stiff attention, and he wasn't alone. Kyle was also hard, and the sight made her pulse speed up. She loved seeing the evidence of what she did to him, and would gladly take a hundred more strokes if it meant he'd fuck her when it was over.

Tom moved around behind her, pulling her wrists together behind her back and holding them tightly in his large hands. The position thrust Megan's full breasts out toward her husband, and forced her to arch her back, pushing her bottom back toward Tom. He crowded close to her and she felt his erection press into her ass. She wanted to grind against it, but she made herself hold still.

Kyle was digging through the Discipline Bag again, and he finally pulled out a short leather whip. Megan moaned, her nipples standing at attention.

Tom pressed himself against her from behind, rubbing his cock against her. His breath came fast and hot against her neck, but Megan kept her attention on her husband. Kyle's cock was visibly straining against his slacks as he shook out the whip and then flicked it toward her.

The short whip was one of Kyle's favorite punishment tools, and he had become a master at controlling it. Megan was literally panting in anticipation, and he didn't disappoint her.

With a flick of his wrist, he teased her clit with it a few times, lightly, just to see her squirm, then moved up to her breasts. The leather snaked out and cracked against her nipples, and Tom's hand immediately clamped around her mouth as she cried out.

"Shhhh," he reminded her.

He kept one hand over her mouth while the other restrained her wrists. As Kyle whipped her breasts again and again, Tom started grunting in her ear, thrusting his cock against her with urgency. Her pale breasts were soon crisscrossed with glowing red stripes, and Kyle teased her every few strokes by letting the leather lick down against her wet pussy.

Megan knew he loved the pattern that the whip made on her skin, and he could have gone on all afternoon decorating her body with it if they had been alone. She could tell that Tom's excitement was distracting her husband, though, and finally Kyle relented and put the whip down.

"Enough," he panted. "What do you need to say to Tom, Megan?"

"Thank you for helping punish me, sir," she said as the other man took his hand off her mouth.

"Would you like a formal thank you, Tom?" Kyle asked politely.

"God, yes," he answered, releasing her wrists and spinning her around to face him.

Megan obediently dropped to her knees as Tom pulled his throbbing cock out in front of her face. She didn't want to disappoint her husband, and silently vowed to make sure that she gave his business partner a memorable blow job.

Reaching out to guide Tom's cock into her mouth, Megan licked the engorged head — slick with precum — and was rewarded by his groan. Tom fisted his hands in her hair as she sucked his length into the back of her mouth.

"She's fantastic," he grunted to Kyle as she used her tongue on him.

Megan smiled around his cock at the praise, and sucked him even harder in response. Reaching out to rub Tom's balls, she gasped as she felt her husband kneel behind her. Kyle reached around her, kneading her breasts and pinching her nipples.

He leaned closer and whispered in her ear: "Deep throat him, Pumpkin, you can do it."

As Kyle continued to pinch and roll her nipples between his fingers, Megan did as she was told. She opened her throat and took Tom's entire cock, not stopping until his balls were pressed against her chin.

"That's it," he moaned above her. "Yessssssssssssss." His grip on her hair tightened painfully and he started guiding her head along the length of his cock more urgently.

Kyle was fumbling with his zipper behind her, and as she continued to let Tom fuck her face she felt her husband's huge cock burst free and press into her from behind. Megan obediently spread her legs, and Kyle forced his shaft up into her tight pussy as she moaned around Tom's cock.

"Fuck!" Tom cried out as her throat muscles vibrated around him. "Again, Megan."

Tom kept control of her head, and Kyle kept his hands firmly on her tits as he fucked her from behind. Megan could let herself go completely as the two men took charge of her, and she moaned for Tom and writhed against her husband as the two hard cocks filled and fucked her.

"Oh *fuck*," Tom yelled out as he suddenly swelled, his heavy cock buried in her throat and threatening to choke her. He slammed his hips into her face as he came. His hot cum pumped down her throat, and Megan managed to swallow all of the salty white seed.

Kyle had been pumping into her in a steady rhythm, but as soon as Tom finished and pulled himself out of her mouth, he pushed her down onto all fours and gripped her hips tightly.

Slamming himself into her in a frenzy, her husband drove his cock deep, again and again, until Megan's whole world narrowed to the feel of his shaft ramming inside her. He'd fucked her hard before, but never like this. Megan wasn't aware of what she was saying or doing, all she knew is that she needed more of him, all of him, or she was going to die.

"Kyle, oh please, harder, *harder, fuck me harder,*" she screamed.

He slapped her red ass as she came, her orgasm swamping her with it's intensity. As soon as her pussy starting pulsing around Kyle's cock, he let out a hoarse shout and filled her with everything he had.

Megan collapsed, naked, wet, and used, on the floor. The two men tidied themselves up as she lay there, trying to catch her breath. She winced when she finally tried to sit up, then smiled. She almost felt guilty for enjoying her punishment so much

"Tom and I have got to get on with our meeting, Pumpkin," Kyle said to her as he helped her up and swatted her butt playfully. "Get yourself cleaned up and head home. I trust you've learned your lesson."

"Yes, sir," she answered as she dressed and gathered her things. Her pussy was still throbbing from that lesson. Suppressing a naughty smile, she turned and asked her husband one last question before she left.

"Will Tom be coming for dinner?"

* * *

SHARING MY WIFE WITH THE COLLEGE-FRIEND

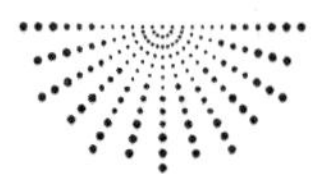

* * *

The blistering sun hung high in the sky, casting a shimmering glow upon the Olympic-sized pool. Isabella stood at the edge, her sleek form clad in a high-tech swimsuit that seemed to hug her every contour. Her coach, not just any coach, but her husband, gazed at her with a mix of pride and intensity.

"Feel the rhythm, Isabella," he called out, his voice cutting through the poolside ambiance. "Each stroke is a note in your symphony."

Isabella nodded, a determined glint in her eyes, and dove into the crystal-clear water. The crowd hushed as she sliced through the surface, a streamlined force of nature. Her husband watched her with an unwavering gaze, his hands gesturing with the precision of a conductor guiding an orchestra.

"Beautiful, love. Extend those arms, feel the water's embrace," he coached, his words a blend of encouragement and expertise.

As Isabella swam, the atmosphere pulsated with a unique energy. Onlookers were drawn not just to the spectacle of Olympic prowess, but to the undeniable connection between athlete and coach. The air was thick with the scent of chlorine, passion, and the unspoken promises that lingered between them.

Amidst the crowd, a figure appeared— Greg, a handsome interloper, Isabella's former competitor, and a friend from her husband's past. He observed the performance with a sly smile, his eyes filled with an enigmatic mix of curiosity and admiration.

Isabella surfaced, water droplets glistening on her skin like liquid diamonds. Her husband approached, a proud grin on his face. "You're a force, Isabella."

She grinned back, her breaths heavy but triumphant. "Your coaching makes all the difference, my love."

The handsome friend sauntered over, a playful smirk on his lips. "Quite the dynamic duo you two make. Mind if I join the party?"

"We're going to Paesano's for dinner after Isabella showers. We'd love to have you, we haven't talked in ages," Michael pat his friend on the back. "We've got some catching up to do. Go get cleaned up, my bathing beauty," Michael tossed his beautiful wife a towel and a wink as she strode to the locker room.

Later, in a private booth at the restaurant, the three friends chatted and laughed over wine and pasta. Greg and Michael shared stories of their college days, while Isabella listened with interest. She observed the two men with a keen eye, noting the easy rapport between them.

"Remember when I won that competition and you threw the big party at your parents' house? The one where you were so drunk that you fell off the diving board and landed on the trampoline?" Greg said, laughing.

Michael grinned sheepishly. "Yeah, my parents were not happy about that."

The two men laughed together, their eyes twinkling. Greg gazed at Michael, his voice softening. "I've missed you. It's been too long since we've talked."

"It has. I've been busy with work, and of course, training Isabella. She's a talented swimmer," Michael replied. He turned to his wife and kissed her cheek, beaming with pride.

"And a beautiful woman" Greg remarked, a hint of admiration in his tone. He paused for a moment, then spoke again. "You're a lucky man, Michael.

Michael smiled, wrapping his arm around his wife. "Yes, I am. Just look at her," Michael cupped Isabella under the chin. "Brains, beauty... and she's such a good student. She really takes instruction well."

Greg glanced at his friend under his brow as Isabella brushed.

"Hey," Michael continued. "Why don't you join us back at our place for a nightcap? We can continue this conversation there."

Greg smiled, his eyes sparkling with interest. "I'd like that. I'd like that very much."

The trio finished a second bottle of wine and after dessert, Greg followed Michael and the beautiful Isabella back to their home.

"You're not going to believe this," Michael whispered to his friend as he showed him into their home.

"What is it?" Greg asked, his eyes filled with curiosity.

"You know that little fantasy I had in college?" Michael responded. "The one with you and me and a girl?"

"The one I helped you act out?" Greg queried, a smirk spreading across his face.

"That's the one," Michael replied. "Well, I think my dear wife Isabella might be up for a little reenactment. But she's a little shy. She might need some encouragement.

Greg grinned, a mischievous glint in his eyes. "Well, you know I'm always up for a challenge."

"Isabella," Michael turned to his wife, "why don't you undress and show my friend Greg your beautiful body?"

"Michael!" Isabella blushed, her cheeks turning red. "You want me to strip in front of your friend?"

"Of course, my love. You're a stunning woman and I want you to feel comfortable with Greg. Come on, off with this," Michael said, pulling down the strap of his wife's dress.

"Michael..." Isabella blushed and turned her gaze to the ground.

"Would you feel more comfortable if I undressed you," Greg interjected. His eyes gleamed with anticipation.

Isabella's glance darted to her husband Michael, who nodded in reply.

"Go ahead," he nodded.

Isabella took a deep breath, then bit her lower lip.

"Be a good girl," Michael admonished her. "Show Greg your beautiful tits. Now."

Greg stepped toward Isabella and gently cupped her chin. "He's right. I'd love to see your gorgeous breasts."

Isabella's breath hitched as Greg's hand slipped under the straps of her dress and slid them down her shoulders. Her breasts bounced out of the top of her dress, exposing her nipples.

"Fuck, she's incredible," Greg murmured, his breath warm against her skin.

"Isn't she gorgeous?" Michael remarked proudly.

"She's stunning," Greg replied, running his fingers over Isabella's nipples, then taking one between his thumb and forefinger and pinching.

Isabella's heart pounded as the handsome men admired her body.

"You're a lucky man," Greg looked over at his friend Michael.

"Oh, I know," Michael grinned.

"So, Isabella," Greg said, turning to the blushing bride. "Your husband tells me that you're quite the good student. That you take instruction well. Is that true?"

Isabella swallowed hard, then nodded. "Yes. I like to please my husband."

"That's good," Greg smiled, trailing a finger down Isabella's neck, over her breastbone, and between the soft mounds of her breasts. "I'd like to help you with that. Would you like me to touch you? To help you please your husband?"

Isabella glanced at her husband for guidance.

"Answer his question, darling," Michael instructed.

"Yes," Isabella breathed. "I'd like that."

"Good girl," Greg said, sliding his hand down Isabella's stomach and slipping it over the front of her panties. His fingers brushed over her mound, then slid between her legs, brushing her lips. He began to stroke it in slow back and forth motions.

Isabella gasped as Greg touched her, her body responding to his skilled hands.

"Why don't we take these off," Greg said, tugging gently at Isabella's panties. She nodded, and he pulled them down, exposing her.

"Turn around, Isabella," Michael commanded. "Let Greg see your tight ass."

Isabella did as she was told, turning slowly.

Greg licked his lips as he gazed at her round cheeks.

"Would you like to touch it?" Michael offered. "She's very soft. Feel for yourself."

"I'd love to," Greg said, his voice low and husky. He ran a hand over Isabella's ass, squeezing it. "It is soft."

"Doesn't she have the most perfect ass you've ever seen?" Michael asked.

Greg nodded in agreement, his fingers tracing the curve of Isabella's cheeks. "She does."

"How about her pussy?" Michael queried, a twinkle in his eye. "Would you like to take a look? Maybe even taste it?"

"Fuck yes," Greg breathed, his eyes dark with desire.

"Turn around and bend over, Isabella," Michael commanded, and his wife gasped. "Greg wants to see your pretty pussy."

Isabella bit her lip as she bent over, exposing herself to her husband's friend.

"That's a good girl," Michael said, running his hand down his wife's back and over her ass. "Take a look at this," he nodded to his friend, pulling his wife's cheeks apart so that Greg could see Isabella's wet lips and tight pink asshole.

Greg licked his lips and reached out, tracing his fingers along the smooth curve of Isabella's ass. "She's a goddess."

"I know," Michael agreed, nodding. "Why don't you take a taste?"

Greg didn't need to be told twice. He knelt down and pressed his lips to Isabella's soft skin, kissing her cheek. Then he licked a line across her ass, tasting her.

Isabella shuddered as Greg's tongue swirled over her skin, leaving a trail of wetness in its wake.

"Mmm, you're delicious," Greg murmured, his breath hot on Isabella's skin. He kissed his way down her ass and over her lips, his tongue dipping into her wet folds. He flicked it across her clit, sending shivers of pleasure through her body.

"Doesn't that feel nice, darling?" Michael asked, watching as his friend tasted his wife.

Isabella nodded, her breathing heavy with desire.

"You like having Greg lick your pussy?" Michael queried, rubbing his hand over Isabella's ass.

"Yes," Isabella gasped.

"Tell him what you want, Isabella," Michael instructed.

"I want him to lick me," Isabella replied, her voice barely above a whisper.

"What was that?" Michael pressed, slapping his wife's ass.

"I want him to lick me," Isabella said, louder this time.

"Louder, my dear," Michael commanded. "Greg can't hear you."

Isabella took a deep breath, her cheeks flushing red with embarrassment. "I want him to lick me. Please."

"That's a good girl," Michael praised, patting her ass gently.

Greg smiled and dipped his head down, burying his face in Isabella's pussy. He licked and sucked at her clit, making her gasp with pleasure. She ground her hips against his face, her body trembling as the sensations grew more intense.

"That's right, my love," Michael said, rubbing Isabella's back. "Enjoy yourself."

Greg's tongue danced over Isabella's clit, bringing her to the edge of orgasm. He lapped at her wetness, his fingers pressing into her thighs. She moaned, her body tensing as she reached her climax.

As Isabella shuddered in ecstasy, Greg pulled back, his lips glistening with her juices. He stood up, his erection straining against his pants.

"Oh dear," Michael tutted. "Isabella, look what you've done to poor Greg. Now what are we going to do about this situation? You should apologize to him for being so naughty."

Isabella glanced over her shoulder at her husband, then down at Greg's tented pants. Her eyes widened in surprise, and she blushed deeply.

"I'm sorry," she whispered, her voice barely audible.

Greg chuckled and unzipped his pants, pulling out his thick, erect cock. "How about you apologize by sucking my cock?"

Isabella gasped as his size, then looked to her husband for guidance.

Michael nodded in approval. "Go ahead, darling. Show Greg how sorry you are."

Isabella turned around and sank to her knees, gazing up at Greg through long, dark lashes. She reached out and wrapped her fingers around his shaft, stroking it gently.

Greg's eyes fluttered shut as she explored his cock. He moaned softly as she traced the length of his shaft with her fingers, feeling every inch of him.

Isabella licked her lips, then leaned forward and flicked her tongue over the tip of Greg's cock, tasting his pre-cum.

"Mmm," she hummed in pleasure.

Greg groaned, his hands tangling in her hair as she wrapped her lips around his shaft and began to suck.

"That's my good girl," Michael murmured, watching his wife pleasure his friend. "Make him feel good."

Isabella bobbed her head up and down on Greg's cock, taking him deeper into her mouth with each stroke. She swirled her tongue around his shaft, teasing him, while her hand pumped the base of his cock.

Greg's breaths came in ragged gasps, his hands fisted in her hair as she worked his cock.

"Not so fast, dear," Michael pulled Isabella back by her hair. "Greedy girl. Why don't you use your tits to make Greg feel good instead?"

"Yes, sir," Isabella breathed, her cheeks flushed. She cupped her breasts and squeezed them together, enveloping Greg's cock in the soft, warm valley of her cleavage.

"Fuck," Greg groaned as Isabella began to move her body up and down, sliding his cock between her breasts. "That feels so fucking good."

Isabella smiled up at him, her eyes sparkling with mischief as she worked his cock. She licked and sucked on the tip whenever it emerged from between her breasts, driving Greg wild.

"Such a talented girl," Michael remarked, stroking Isabella's hair.

"She sure is," Greg panted, thrusting his hips forward, his cock sliding between Isabella's tits.

"Would you like to feel how tight my wife is? You can have her pussy if you'd like," Michael offered, smirking.

"You wouldn't mind?" Greg asked, a surprised look on his face.

"Of course not. You're our guest," Michael replied. "And you've been so kind as to help me train Isabella. I'm sure she'd enjoy it."

"Then I'd be honored," Greg said, his voice thick with desire.

"Isabella, show Greg how much you want him," Michael instructed.

Isabella stood up and turned around, bending over and spreading her legs wide. She reached back and spread her cheeks, revealing her dripping pussy and tight asshole.

Greg's cock twitched at the sight. "Fuck," he breathed. "She's incredible."

"Isn't she?" Michael said, smiling proudly. "Now, why don't you go ahead and fuck her? Show her what you can do."

"Gladly," Greg responded, stepping forward and rubbing the tip of his cock against Isabella's wet pussy. He teased her clit with his shaft, making her gasp. Then he thrust forward, plunging into her depths.

Isabella cried out as Greg filled her, his thick cock stretching her tight hole.

Greg's thrusts were slow and steady, and he moaned as her walls gripped his cock. "Fuck, you're so tight."

"I love the way you're stretching her," Michael murmured, watching his friend fuck his wife. "I think she loves it too."

Isabella whimpered in agreement, her body trembling with pleasure as Greg pounded into her. She gasped as he reached forward, squeezing and playing with her breasts. Her eyes met her husband's and she blushed with shame, getting fucked so hard right in front of her husband.

Greg sped up his thrusts, pounding Isabella's pussy with abandon. "Your wife feels incredible," he panted.

Michael grinned, his hand snaking down to his pants. "She does, doesn't she?"

"Mmhmm," Greg groaned, gripping Isabella's hips and pulling her onto his cock. He plunged into her depths, over and over, his body slapping against hers.

As Greg and Isabella's bodies joined in a passionate embrace, Michael unzipped his pants and pulled out his cock. He began to stroke himself as he watched his wife and friend fuck.

Isabella's cries of pleasure grew louder as Greg's thrusts became more powerful. She arched her back, pushing her ass against him, trying to take his cock deeper inside her.

Greg gripped Isabella's hips and slammed into her, his balls slapping against her ass.

Isabella screamed in ecstasy as she came, her pussy clenching around Greg's cock. Her body shuddered, her legs trembling.

Greg grunted, his thrusts becoming more erratic. He fucked Isabella hard and fast, chasing his own release.

"Are you close, friend?" Michael asked, his hand stroking his cock faster.

"Fuck yes," Greg moaned, his hips jerking as he pumped into Isabella.

"Come in her, Greg. Fill her up," Michael encouraged.

"Yes, sir," Greg replied, his body tensing as he reached the edge of orgasm. His cock throbbed inside Isabella and then he exploded, shooting his load deep inside her pussy.

Isabella whimpered as Greg filled her, her body trembling with pleasure.

"That's a good girl," Michael murmured, his eyes locked on his wife and friend. "Take it all."

Greg groaned as he emptied himself into Isabella. His cock throbbed inside her, his body shuddering.

Isabella panted, her chest heaving as she struggled to catch her breath.

As Greg and Isabella's bodies came down from their high, Michael stepped forward, his cock hard and ready.

"Isabella, I think you're forgetting something," he chided, rubbing the tip of his cock against her tight asshole. "It's only polite to reciprocate. Greg fucked your pussy, but your ass still belongs to me."

Isabella gasped as her husband rubbed his cock against her asshole. "Michael! I-I don't know if I can..."

"You can, and you will," Michael insisted. "I want you to take my cock like a good little girl. Greg made you feel good, now it's time for you to make me feel good too."

"Is he... is he going to watch?" Isabella's eyes darted to Greg, who was still catching his breath.

"Of course," Michael grinned. "And you're going to show him how well you take my cock. How much you love it when I fuck your tight little hole.

Isabella blushed and nodded, spreading her cheeks again for her husband.

Michael smirked and lined his cock up with Isabella's tight hole, slowly pressing into her. He watched as her asshole stretched to accommodate his girth, his cock sinking deeper into her depths.

Isabella gasped as Michael entered her, her body quivering. She bit her lip as he began to thrust, his cock filling her.

Greg watched, mesmerized, as Michael's cock slid in and out of Isabella's ass. He stroked his cock back to hardness, enjoying the sight.

Michael grunted as he fucked Isabella's tight hole, his balls slapping against her ass. "Such a good girl," he breathed, his hands gripping her hips. "Taking my cock so well. Look at how much Isabella loves having her tight little asshole fucked by her husband," he turned to his friend.

"She's incredible," Greg murmured, stroking his cock faster.

Isabella whimpered as Michael slammed into her, his cock stretching her ass. She pushed back against him, meeting each thrust.

"You're a natural at this, Isabella," Michael panted. "I think you should give Greg another blowjob while I fuck you."

Isabella nodded, her eyes wide with arousal.

"That's my girl," Michael smiled, pulling out of her ass. "Come here."

Isabella moved over to Greg, sinking down to her knees. She licked her lips and gazed up at him through hooded eyes.

Greg groaned, his cock throbbing. "Please."

Isabella grinned and took Greg's cock into her mouth, sucking eagerly.

"Fuck," Greg moaned, tangling his fingers in Isabella's hair.

Michael watched, his cock twitching at the sight of his wife sucking Greg's cock.

Isabella bobbed her head up and down on Greg's shaft, her tongue swirling around the tip. She hollowed her cheeks and sucked hard, drawing a moan of pleasure from him.

Greg's eyes fluttered shut as Isabella pleasured him, his hips thrusting forward involuntarily.

Isabella moaned as she tasted Greg's cock, her eyes darting back to meet her husband, who was lining the head of his cock back up with her tender asshole. She let out a muffled cry as Michael's cock pushed back into her tight hole.

"Take it, Isabella," Michael grunted as he thrust into her. "You love having your asshole fucked, don't you?"

Isabella grunted, her mouth full of Greg's cock.

Greg's breaths came in short, ragged gasps as he fucked Isabella's mouth, his eyes locked on her husband.

Michael grinned and slapped Isabella's ass, watching as her cheeks bounced. "What a good little girl you are, taking my cock in your ass and Greg's cock in your mouth," he grunted as he fucked her, his balls slapping against her skin.

Isabella's body rocked between the two men, their cocks sliding in and out of her holes. She moaned, her body tingling with pleasure.

Michael's thrusts became more erratic as he neared his climax. He pounded into Isabella's ass, his balls slapping against her skin. "Fuck, I'm gonna cum," he grunted, his cock throbbing inside her.

Isabella moaned, her body trembling as Michael filled her ass with his hot seed.

Greg groaned, his cock pulsating as he erupted inside Isabella's mouth. His cum dripped down her chin as he pulled out, a satisfied grin on his face.

Isabella swallowed, licking her lips clean. Her body shuddered as she came, her pussy clenching around nothing.

"That's a good girl," Michael praised, rubbing her back as he pulled out of her. "You did such a good job for us."

Isabella blushed and looked up at her husband with a shy smile.

Michael smiled back at her, then turned to Greg. "Well, that was quite the performance," he said with a chuckle. "Thank you for indulging us, old friend. I trust this will not be the last time?"

Greg smirked, running his fingers through his hair. "You can count on it. Your wife is incredible."

"She certainly is," Michael replied, smiling down at Isabella.

"I'd better be going, though," Greg said, tucking his spent cock back into his pants. "Thanks again for the show."

"Anytime," Michael grinned. "Goodnight, Greg. See you soon."

"See you soon," Greg echoed, heading out the door and leaving Michael and Isabella alone.

"Well, my dear," Michael said, turning to his wife. "I think that was a very successful lesson, don't you?"

Isabella blushed, a shy smile spreading across her face. "It was... exciting. Thank you for sharing me with Greg, Michael."

"Of course," Michael replied, stroking her cheek. "You're a beautiful woman, Isabella. I want you to experience all the pleasures of the flesh. And I'm happy to share you with my friends."

"You are an amazing husband," Isabella breathed, her eyes sparkling with love and lust.

"And you are an amazing wife," Michael responded, kissing her deeply.

* * *

SHARING MY WIFE BEFORE THE WEDDING

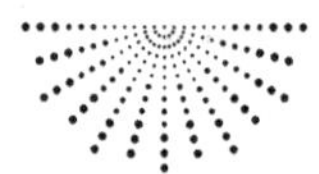

* * *

When Laura arrived at the attorney's office she wasn't sure what to expect. A pre-nup? Dean had been pretty close mouthed about the purpose of the appointment, but he'd also made it clear that this meeting was non-negotiable.

It was two days before their wedding, and Laura was full of first time bride jitters. It had been a whirlwind romance with the wedding scheduled just four months after their first date. Some of Laura's friends were a little skeptical about her decision to make a lifelong commitment to a man after such a short period of time, but Laura had no doubts.

From the moment she'd met Dean, she was smitten. He was unlike any guy she'd ever dated. When she was with him she wanted to be a better person, and Dean fully supported her efforts to better herself. He was always sure of himself, and she felt calm and confident when she was with him, knowing that he would take care of any situation that came up.

During their second date, Laura had made a self deprecating comment about her bad habit of running late. She had kept Dean waiting for ten minutes when he'd arrived to pick her up.

"Do you want to change that, Laura?" he'd asked her in a serious tone.

"Of course I'd *like* to," Laura had laughed. "But Dean, I was born late, and I've been late for everything for the last 23 years. If I haven't been able to get my act together by now I just don't see how it's going to happen!"

"You just need someone to hold you accountable, baby," Dean had replied with a warm smile. "I would love to be that someone."

Laura had fallen a little bit in love with him then, and the feeling had only grown. Everyone else in her life seemed to accept her flaws, but Dean was constantly encouraging her to overcome them.

It wasn't long after he proposed that he sat her down and talked to her about basing their marriage on a Domestic Discipline lifestyle. Laura had never heard of such a thing, but the idea that Dean would always be the Head of their Household made sense.

Whether it was holding doors for her, ordering for her at restaurants, or steering her decisions with her 401k, Dean had guided their relationship with a firm hand from the beginning. Laura trusted him completely, and his willingness to take responsibility for her was a kind of freedom she hadn't know before.

Dean made it clear that their marriage would include her submitting to his leadership in all things. She was to listen to him at all times, treat him with respect, and obey him at all times.

When Dean had arrived to pick her up for their next date, Laura was, of course, not quite ready. When she finally finished putting herself together she expected them to rush out the door immediately to make their dinner reservation. Instead, she got her first taste of accountability from the man she was planning on marrying.

"I've cancelled our reservations, Laura," he'd told her quietly.

"We're not that late, honey," she'd laughed as she started to head out the door. "Don't be silly! We can still make it."

Dean reached over her and pushed the door closed firmly. Looking up at him in surprise, Laura realized that something else was going on.

"Were you serious when you told me that you wanted to change your habit of tardiness, baby?"

Laura nodded. His sober demeanor was giving her butterflies in her stomach. She really, really hoped she hadn't messed up with the man she loved.

"Then it's my job to hold you accountable. Do you trust me to do that in the way that I see fit?"

Really nervous now, Laura nodded again. Dean walked over and sat on the edge of her small loveseat. Patting his knee, he motioned her toward him.

"I love you, baby, and I want to support you in bettering yourself. The only way to do that is to punish behavior that you want to stop," he said reasonably. "You're going to come bend over my knee, and I'm going to give you a spanking. I know it's going to hurt you, and I need you to trust that I'm doing it because I love you. The spanking is your punishment for being late. So any pain that you feel, I need you to realize that it's the pain caused by your constant tardiness. Can you do that?"

Laura hesitated, but decided to trust him. This was the man who she was going to spend the rest of her life with, and she had promised to listen, respect, and obey him in all things. She swallowed hard as she realized that she'd put herself in a situation where that promise was really being put to the test.

Laying herself over his bended knee, she sucked in a sharp breath as he pulled her short skirt up to her waist. When he pulled her lacy thong down to fully expose her, she wondered if the whole spanking thing was a joke, and just his way of getting her naked instead of going out to dinner. She smiled a little as she felt a warm tingle of moisture in her pussy. She wouldn't really mind that--

Smack!

Laura cried out in pain as his hand landed on her bare ass. This was no joke. His hand landed on her tender flesh again and again, until it felt like it was on fire and she started to wiggle away from the blows.

"Laura!" Dean reprimanded her sharply. "Obey!"

Sniffling, with tears running down her cheeks, Laura held herself as still as she could while he worked over her bare ass and upper thighs with hard, stinging whacks. She had never been hit in her life, and had never felt anything like the burning, fiery pain that coursed through her lower body.

Finally, it was over. Laura lay across his lap sobbing as Dean tenderly massaged her painful, red skin.

"I'm proud of you, baby," he told her softly. "I know that was hard, but you were able to take it. And I truly hope it will help you remember to plan ahead better in the future so you're not late. Especially now that you know what the consequences will be."

He lifted her up in his arms and kissed her tenderly. After she calmed down, he took her in the bedroom and gently undressed her. Laying her down on the bed on her stomach, he rubbed a soothing lotion onto her cherry red skin. Pulling a decorative cylindrical pillow from the head of her bed, he told her to lift her hips and then slid it beneath her hips.

"Open your legs, baby."

She did as she was told, trying to ignore the lingering pain from her spanking.

"Let me show you that obeying me is worth it," he whispered before kneeling between her legs. Gasping, she felt his hot tongue stroke her cunt firmly. Using his hands to spread her legs wider, Dean lapped at her moisture as she moaned in pleasure. Using his tongue to thrust inside her, he slid one hand under her hot pussy so that he could stroke her swollen clit.

"Dean!" she gasped, close to coming already.

"Up on your knees," he ordered.

As soon as she was in position, he pushed his thick cock into her needy slit. As he thrust into her, Laura cried out at the pleasure/pain from the erotic friction inside and the abrasion against her fiery skin. It felt amazing, but she still found herself pulling away from him to protect her painful rump.

"You will obey me in all things, Laura," he reminded her sharply with a hard smack to her stinging skin.

Tears sprang to her eyes as she dug her hands into the bed cover and held still for his pounding thrusts. He slipped his hand under her again and rubbed against her clit as he drove himself into her.

"Are you going to obey, no matter what?" Dean asked hoarsely.

"Yes, sir," she replied breathlessly.

"Then *come*, Laura. *Now*," he ordered as he slammed into her one last time. Her pussy clenched around his hard cock as he pumped his cum deep into her fertile body. The waves of ecstasy that pulsed through her were stronger than anything she had felt before, and as Dean collapsed on top of her burning skin Laura smiled in contentment at what he had taught her.

Laura would *always* obey.

As they walked into the attorney's office together, she thought back to that first spanking and smiled at the memory. Little had she known how much time she would spend with a sore bottom, but of course Dean had been correct. It was *always* worth it.

He had helped her change and correct so many things already and she couldn't wait for their wedding the day after tomorrow, and her chance to formally pledge herself to him forever.

Once they were seated, the attorney handed her a contract to review. Instead of a pre-nup, is was a different type of agreement.

"What *is* this, honey?" she asked Dean in confusion.

"Laura, I asked Mr. White to draw up a formal agreement between us that outlines the rules in our relationship. I know you don't enjoy being punished--"

Laura blushed furiously. She couldn't believe he would bring up their private activities in front of a stranger. Dean saw her embarrassment and smiled softly.

"Baby, I'm sure Mr. White has seen and heard it all and keeps it all under strict attorney-client privilege. And truly, you have nothing to be embarrassed about. Your willingness to submit to my authority is something any man would be envious of."

The attorney nodded in agreement as Dean continued.

"Please consider these written rules a sort of love letter, from me to you. After all, if you don't know the rules then you might accidentally break them. I'm hoping that if we have a clear agreement, you'll be able to avoid punishment in the future."

Laura looked down at the document in her hand and nodded. He was right. Of course. She reached for a pen to sign the formal contract requiring her to be a submissive wife, but Dean's hand on her wrist stopped her.

"Laura, please read it over carefully so that you really know what you're agreeing to."

For once, Laura asserted herself and shook off his hand.

"Dean," she said confidently. "I don't need to read it. I'll happily sign it and abide by the rules that are outlined here, because above all, I vow to obey you in *all things.*"

Dean smiled down at her with pride as she signed her maiden name for the last time.

* * *

On the morning of her wedding, Laura woke up early, having finally broken the habit of being late thanks to Dean's support. She hummed in happiness as she stepped out of the shower and thought about what she needed to do before leaving for the church later that morning.

Wrapping a towel around her, she walked out of the bathroom and squealed in surprise at the sight of Dean standing in the middle of her bedroom.

"Honey, you know it's bad luck to see me before the wedding," she said with a smile as she went up on her tiptoes and kissed him. Kissing her back enthu-siastically, he pulled her closer and she felt the bulge of his cock swelling against her stomach.

"Ahem."

Startled, Laura squealed and pushed herself closer to Dean as she turned her head to look over her shoulder.

"Hi, Laura," Dean's brother Daniel said with a sheepish smile.

"What…?" Laura pulled the bath towel tighter around her body as she looked back and forth between the two brothers. Finally deciding it was Dean who owed her an explanation, she faced him and asked the obvious question.

"Dean, what are you guys doing here?"

"Sit down, baby," he said while motioning toward her bed.

Instead, Laura pulled away and headed for her closet. She couldn't believe Daniel was still standing in her bedroom while she wore nothing but a bath towel.

"Let me just get some clothes--"

"Laura!" Dean said sharply as he grabbed her arm. "Are you disobeying me?"

Blushing, Laura looked down and then shook her head. Dean had proven to her time and again that he knew what was best, so despite her discomfort at being practically naked in front of her future brother-in-law she went and sat quietly on the edge of the bed. To her surprise, Daniel took a seat on her vanity bench instead of leaving the room.

"Laura, I came over here to talk to you about obedience, and the first thing that you do is defy me," Dean said with disappointment in his voice.

Laura's head came up sharply. She wanted to argue, but she held her tongue. He was right. Once he could see that she wasn't going to talk back, Dean smiled approvingly and continued.

"Baby, first I want you to know how much I love you, and how happy I am that we're going to be man and wife later today."

Laura's heart glowed at the happy thought.

"Once we're married, you will be mine completely," he reminded her. "But I *have to know* whether I can truly count on you to do my will in all things. No matter what."

"Dean!" Laura burst out. "Of course you can!" She felt that she'd proven her willingness to obey him, time and again. Why did he insist on doubting her?

"Baby, I have to know," he said softly, forgiving her outburst with a smile. "Daniel is here because he's the only man on earth I trust enough to help me test you. Are you willing to prove your ultimate obedience to me right now, before we take our vows?"

"Yes, sir," Laura said softly.

She didn't know what he was talking about, but the serious look on his face made her belly tighten with nervous tension. She realized that he needed to have absolute confidence in her before taking her as his wife, and she vowed that whatever he required of her this morning she would submit to completely.

Dean smiled in relief at her answer. He walked over and tenderly kissed her lips before trading places with Daniel. As Dean took a seat, Daniel walked over and stood in front of Laura, blocking her view of her fiancé.

"Laura," Dean directed from behind his brother. "You disobeyed me a few minutes ago, and for that you've earned a spanking. Please remove your towel and lay over the edge of the bed so that Daniel can punish you on my behalf."

Mortified, Laura almost hesitated. Then she unwrapped the large towel with shaking hands and turned to bend over the bed, her bare ass exposed to her future brother-in-law and her large breasts swinging beneath her.

Laura squeezed her eyes closed tightly. She couldn't believe Dean was asking this of her, and that he was willing to have his brother see and touch her naked body. Tensing for her spanking, she reminded herself that she trusted Dean absolutely.

Daniel had probably never spanked anyone in his life, Laura thought with a small smile as his bare hand landed gently on her tender skin. Although she never enjoyed being punished, Laura had to hold back the giggles as Daniel lightly smacked one cheek and then the other. She suspected that he was getting a little distracted by her nakedness, and secretly, she admitted that the bizarre situation was turning her on, as well.

With every swat, Daniel's hand seemed to linger on her skin. Pretty soon he was doing more than linger, as he started letting his fingers glide into the crack of her ass and down lower, over the plump pink flesh of her pussy. The first time it happened Laura tensed. She didn't know whether Dean could see what his brother was doing, but she couldn't imagine he would be ok with such intimate touching.

Dean remained silent, and Laura soon forgot to worry about it as Daniel gave up all pretense of spanking her and simply let himself caress her ass and rub her pussy. She tried to remain still, but his forbidden touch and the knowledge that Dean was watching and not stopping him soon had her panting and moaning with need.

Laura was as confused as she was horny. She knew Dean was a traditionalist, and she wasn't sure what he expected from her. Did he want her to simply obey his command and give his brother full access to her body, or was he waiting for her to pull away from Daniel and put a stop to his advances? She knew it was a test, and she was deathly afraid of failing.

Her pussy was so wet now that all three of them could hear the sloppy, erotic sound of Daniel touching her. He held her ass cheeks open with one hand and stroked and fingered her with the other. Laura couldn't hold herself still any more and was thrusting her hips back toward him and rubbing herself harder against his large, callused fingers.

"Dean!" she finally sobbed. She needed to know what he meant for her to do. She was close to coming, and she could hear Daniel's heavy breathing as he worked her into a frenzy. There was no way Dean could fail to see what was happening, but he hadn't said a word since ordering her to take the spanking from his brother.

"Daniel," Dean finally said in a strained voice. "Please take your hands off my future wife."

Laura almost cried in frustration. She had been on the verge of coming, and even though she knew it was wrong, getting interrupted when she was so close made her want to scream.

"Laura, turn around and suck Daniel's cock."

Shocked, Laura stood up and looked at Dean. Daniel had taken a couple of steps to the side and stood there panting, as his hot gaze roamed over her peaked nipples, sleek curves, and smooth, shaved mound.

"Don't make me repeat myself, baby," Dean said in the same strained voice. "If you plan on obeying me, then *obey.*"

Nodding jerkily, Laura turned toward Daniel and fell to her knees. Daniel's cock was straining against the soft material of his pants, and she could see a wet spot where his precum had soaked through the cloth. The site made her clench her thighs as a spike of desire shot through her.

Without waiting to lower his pants, Laura wrapped her hot mouth around the head of his cock, sucking and licking it through the material. Bracing one hand on Daniel's hip, she used her other hand to stroke the thick, hot shaft through his pants.

"Oh my God!" Daniel groaned. Fumbling at his waistband, he pushed her off of him for a moment and shoved his shorts and briefs down to his thighs. Grabbing the back of her head, he jammed his bare cock back into her mouth and threw his head back as she wrapped her tongue around his sensitive head and then sucked him, hard, in and out of her hot, wet cavity.

"Don't come in her mouth, bro," Dean said suddenly.

Laura felt the familiar weight of her fiancé's hands on her shoulders as he came up behind her and stroked her bare skin. He was standing so close that she could feel the nudge of his erection press into the back of her head as she bobbed over his brother's cock.

"I don't know if I can, stop, Dean," Daniel panted. "She is fucking *awesome.*"

"Laura, stop," Dean ordered.

Beyond questioning, Laura did as she was told. Holding utterly still, she kneeled between the two men with Daniel's twitching cock laying across her tongue.

"For God's sake, Danny," Dean said with an edgy laugh. "Take your cock out of her mouth!"

Once he did, Dean told her to lay back on the bed with her ass at the edge. Dean planted himself between her legs and lifted her feet up to his shoulders. Pulling his own cock out, he shoved it into her and buried himself to the hilt with a harsh groan.

"God, baby," he managed to say. "You are *so hot.*"

Laura tried to brace herself as Dean pounded into her like a madman. He had never taken her so hard, and after the first few thrusts he had to grab the tops of her thighs to keep her from getting shoved farther up the bed as he drove into her.

Immediately, her whole body tensed and she came in hot waves that made her sheath pulse around Dean's cock. He paused to watch her, then looked back at his brother.

"Daniel," he finally ground out. "Come join me."

As Dean paused, Daniel took one of Laura's legs and pulled it open wider so that he could stand next to his brother. Sweat broke out on Dean's brow as he held himself back long enough for Daniel to insert a finger next to Dean's cock, inside Laura's tight cunt. Daniel used his finger to work her open wide enough that he could push the head of his dick in next to his brother's.

As the second cock slowly slid into her, Laura didn't know if she could take it. The painful stretching was worse than the fiery pain of her first spanking. Without meaning to, she started to scramble back as both Daniel and Dean forced their thick rods into her at the same time.

"Laura!" Dean reprimanded her sharply.

"I'm sorry, honey," she panted as she forced herself to stay still and let her pussy adjust to the double fucking.

After sitting on the sidelines and watching earlier, Dean was barely able to hold himself back. As soon as Daniel managed to get his thick dick all the way in, Dean lunged forward, driving his own cock in next to his brother's. The two brothers each had their cocks buried to the hilt in her wet, wet pussy and Laura felt so full she thought she was going to burst. As they started to thrust into her in an alternating rhythm, the friction became too much. Too good.

Thankful for the firm grip they had on her thighs, she frantically reached her hand down to find her clit, moaning loudly as the two men fucked her. Closing her eyes to focus on the waves of pleasure, Laura had no idea who came first, but when she felt the hot burst of the two brothers' cum pump into her cunt she was rocked with a second, massive orgasm.

Spent, Laura lay back on the bed with her eyes closed. Listening to the murmur of their voices, Laura couldn't believe what had just happened. It had been the most amazing sex of her life. Once again, Dean had proven to her that obeying his authority was always the right choice.

When she heard her bedroom door close softly, she opened her eyes and sat up. She was alone with Dean, and he was smiling down at her lovingly as he cleaned himself up.

"Daniel just left, baby, and I've got to go get ready for the ceremony," he reached down and tenderly kissed the top of her head. "Your obedience in front of my brother made me so proud."

Laura smiled happily as he walked out. She couldn't wait to walk down the aisle toward him later that day. Now that he truly believed it, she wanted everyone to hear her promise her obedience to the man she loved.

Humming happily, she wondered what he would require of her for her wedding night.

* * *

GET A FREE BOOK!

* * *

Be the first to find out about all of Lee Riley's new releases, book sales, and freebies by joining her VIP Mailing List. Join today and get a FREE book -- instantly!

Check Lee Riley's website spicybestsellers.com for more books.

* * *

ABOUT LEE RILEY

* * *

Lee Riley is an adventurous writer who creates spicy short stories that challenge conventions and leave readers on the edge of their seats. Drawing inspiration from their travels, Lee explores the world with insatiable curiosity, using these experiences to craft stories that captivate readers.

When not writing, Lee indulges their passion for the outdoors, discovering new culinary delights, and making connections with people from all walks of life. Their love for adventure and zest for life is reflected in their work, which is daring, unconventional, and full of surprises.

More on www.spicybestsellers.com

Contact me at lee@spicybestsellers.com

* * *

LEE RILEY
Daddy's Naughty Girls 2
DEVOURED
BY HER STEPFATHER

LEE RILEY
Daddy's Naughty Girls 3
UNDRESSED
BY HER STEPFATHER

DOMESTIC DISCIPLINE ROMANCE

LEE RILEY
6 Books!
One Price!
BACK ALLEY
DISCIPLINE
DOMESTIC DISCIPLINE
BUNDLE

LEE RILEY
5 Books!
One Price!
BACK DOOR
DISCIPLINE
DOMESTIC DISCIPLINE
BUNDLE

LEE RILEY
6 Books! One Price!
GET PUNISHED
DOMESTIC DISCIPLINE BUNDLE

LEE RILEY
6 Books! One Price!
GET SPANKED
DOMESTIC DISCIPLINE BUNDLE

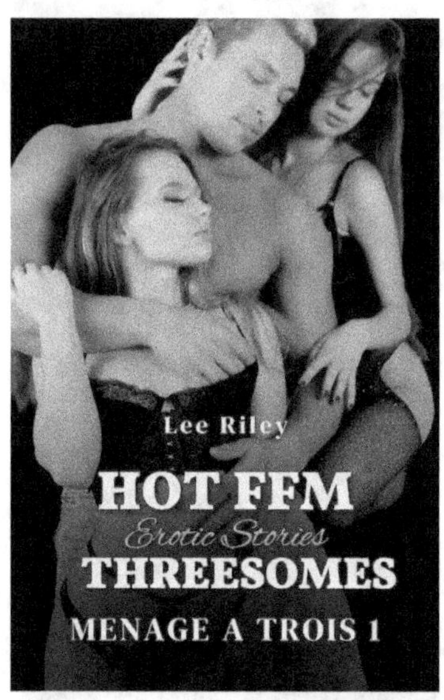
Lee Riley
HOT FFM
Erotic Stories
THREESOMES
MENAGE A TROIS 1

Lee Riley
WILD FFM
Erotic Stories
THREESOMES
MENAGE A TROIS 2

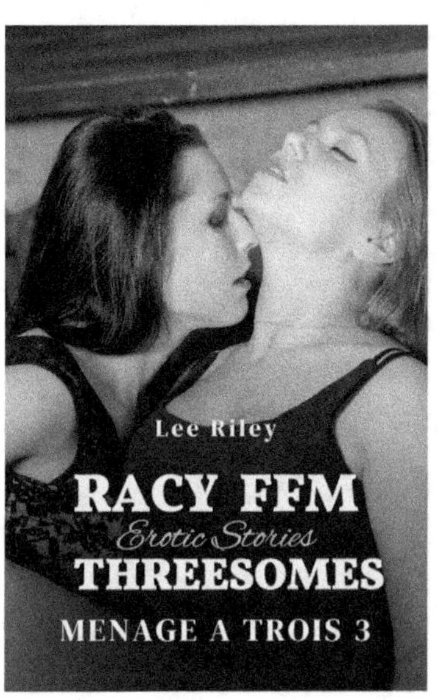

MONSTER EROTICA

LEE RILEY
MONSTROUS ENCOUNTERS
WEREWOLVES
3 Books!
One Price!
Seductive Creatures 2

LEE RILEY
MONSTROUS ENCOUNTERS
DEMONESSES
3 Books!
One Price!
Seductive Creatures 3

LEE RILEY
MONSTROUS ENCOUNTERS
TENTACLES & GRIM REAPER
3 Books! One Price!
Seductive Creatures 4

LEE RILEY
MONSTROUS ENCOUNTERS
KRAMPUS
Seductive Creatures 5

LEE RILEY
THE DEMON
KING
LITRPG EROTICA STORIES

* * *